P9-EGL-356

PHANTOM OF THE OPERA

Illustrated by
Greg Hildebrandt

Adapted from the novel by
Gaston Leroux

BARNES
&NOBLE
BOOKS
NEW YORK

Phantom Of The Opera

Into the dressing room of Madame Sorelli, one of the main dancers, rushed half a dozen young ladies of the ballet. They rushed in amid great confusion, some chattering, others laughing nervously, and still others with cries of terror. It was some time before they could be understood clearly.

"It's the ghost!" shrieked the smallest girl in the group.

"Have you seen him?" demanded Sorelli.

"As plainly as I see you now!" cried the girl.

"If it was the ghost, he's very ugly!" added another girl.

"Oh, yes!" cried the chorus of ballet-girls.

And they all began to talk at once. The ghost had appeared to them in the shape of a gentleman in dress-clothes, who had suddenly appeared in the passageway. He seemed to have come straight through the wall.

"Pooh!" said Sorelli. "You girls see the ghost everywhere!"

And it was true. For several months, there had been nothing discussed at the Paris Opera but this ghost in dress-clothes who stalked about the building like a shadow. The ghost spoke to no one, and no one dared speak to him. As soon as he was seen, he would vanish without a trace. If anyone met with a fall, or suffered a practical joke at the hands of a friend, or lost a powder puff, it was at once the fault of the ghost. Those who had seen him described his appearance as that of a skeleton, with two dead black holes for eyes.

It was the evening on which Mr. Debienne and Mr. Poligny, the managers of the Opera, were giving a last gala performance to mark their retirement. Everyone who was anyone in Paris high society was in attendance that evening.

The triumph of the night, by far, was delivered by Christine Daae, a hitherto unknown singer to the Opera. She had taken the place of La Carlotta, who had become ill that evening. Christine performed in *Faust* as the beautiful Margarita. She revealed a new Margarita that night, a Margarita of a splendor, a radiance hitherto unsuspected. The whole house went mad, rising to its feet, shouting and cheering, while Christine sobbed and fainted in the arms of a fellow singer. She had to be carried away at once to her dressing room.

Not everyone was cheering, though. In a private box above the stage, the well-respected Count of Chagny, Philippe, sat with his younger brother, Raoul. It was Raoul who did not clap or shout, but rather turned pale and trembled. For Raoul was in love with Christine Daae, ever since they were children, and seeing her faint onstage had sent him into a panic. Raoul made straightaway for her dressing room to assure himself that his beloved Christine was all right. To his shock and surprise, his childhood friend would not see him! Raoul had been away in the navy for some time. Had she found another man in his absence? And her voice! He did not think she was capable of such beauty. And why had she fainted away like that? The questions burned within him. He remained hidden in the shadows just outside her door until the doctor and maid left her alone. He was determined to speak to her that night.

Hardly breathing, he went up to the dressing room, and, with his ear to the door to catch her reply, he prepared to knock. But his hand dropped. He heard a man's voice in the dressing room, saying, "Christine, you must love me!"

And Christine's voice, sad and trembling, replied:

"How can you talk like that? *When I only sing for you!*"

Raoul leaned against the door to ease his pain. What a position for the young count to be in! Lurking in hallways and listening behind doors! The man's voice spoke again:

"Are you very tired?"

"Oh, tonight I gave you my soul, and I am dead!"

"Your soul is a beautiful thing, child," replied the man's voice, "and I thank you. No emperor ever received so fair a gift. *The angels wept tonight.*"

Raoul heard nothing after that. Ashamed and hurt, he quietly went away, determined he would speak to her at the earliest possible moment.

Later that night, in the Grand Ballroom of the Opera, the retiring managers held a wonderful dinner to toast their departure. At this dinner a very unusual guest was in attendance.

"The Opera ghost!" came the hushed cries around the table.

There sat the ghost, as natural as could be, except he neither ate nor drank. The only difference in his appearance than on previous sightings was the fact that he had a nose. But for those who dared to look, it was obvious that the nose was not real. He sat at the end of the table for some time; few ventured to look at the ghost, and none spoke a word to him for fear of offending this visitor from the tomb. Without anyone seeing him leave, the ghost was suddenly gone! Vanished! Had the guests that night only dreamed they had seen the ghost? The departing managers knew better. For they, more than most, *knew* the ghost.

After dinner, the departing managers met with Mr. Richard and Mr. Moncharmin, the incoming managers, in their office.

"Well, gentlemen," Mr. Moncharmin began, "everything appears to be in order. Is there anything else you wish to relate before you both begin a happy and restful retirement?"

Both Mr. Debienne and Mr. Poligny were quite pale, and the two men looked nervously at each other.

"There is one—one more matter to discuss, gentlemen," Mr. Debienne said gravely. "That is the matter of the Opera ghost."

"The ghost? You jest, surely?" Mr. Richard said, laughing.

"The ghost is no joke, I assure you," warned Mr. Debienne sternly. "And the ghost has demands. Demands you gentlemen would be wise to meet."

"Demands?" asked Mr. Richard jokingly.

"Yes, gentlemen," continued Mr. Debienne. "The ghost requires that Box Five be placed at his disposal for every performance. In addition, a payment of twenty thousand francs is to be left in Box Five at the first of every month. That comes to exactly two hundred and forty thousand francs a year."

The two new managers held back their laughter until the former managers had departed.

"Twenty thousand francs! Well, this ghost certainly has expensive tastes!" Mr. Richard howled with laughter.

"And he is quite a devoted patron of the Opera, I must say," shot back Mr. Moncharmin, "needing a box every night!"

They thought the former managers were playing a superb joke. Over the next four days they became less and less amused. Several notes came to their office from the supposed "Opera ghost," demanding his payment and warning that Box Five must not be sold. The new managers thought the joke was being carried a bit too far, and ordered Box Five to be sold for every performance. The ghost warned again that they should make payment swiftly, or be prepared for disaster. The managers' anger turned to fear and horror the fifth night. The ghost had his revenge.

They had decided to take seats in Box Five themselves for a performance of *Faust* with La Carlotta as Margarita. In the middle of her performance, a voice spoke in Box Five (yet the managers saw no one), saying, *"She is singing tonight to bring the chandelier down!"* At that moment, the grand chandelier, the massive chandelier, came crashing down upon the audience.

Christine Daae had gone into hiding since her astonishing performance the week before. Raoul was desperate to speak with her. He made inquiries all over Paris as to her whereabouts. He had all but given up hope when he received a letter, which read:

MONSIEUR,

I have not forgotten the little boy who now is a man that has always been my friend. I feel I must write you to tell you that I am in the village of Perros, in fulfillment of a sacred duty. Tomorrow is the anniversary of the death of my poor father. He is buried there, with his violin, in the graveyard of the little church, beside the road where we said good-bye as children for the last time. CHRISTINE.

An ominous feeling swept over Raoul, and he made his way at once to the railway station, where he took the next train to Perros. The train did not arrive till nightfall, but he wasted no time, and went to the home of Christine's aunt, where he was sure she was staying.

To his surprise, he was told she had gone to the churchyard at sunset, and had yet to return. Raoul climbed the small hill on which the church was built. The moon was full and high in the sky, so it didn't take him long to spot Christine kneeling by her father's grave. But as he approached her, the air suddenly filled with the sound of music—beautiful, beguiling, bewitching music.

Raoul stepped back and hid himself as Christine rose and turned in the direction of the music. The enchanted yet profoundly tragic notes sang out from the strings of a violin. Raoul's eyes tried to pierce the dark recesses of the church archway from which the music was coming. But of the mysterious musician he could see nothing. When the music stopped, Christine quietly left the graveyard and returned down the hill. Raoul acted at once, and ran to the archway to uncover the source of the midnight melody. In an instant he stood before a nightmare—a horrible, horrible nightmare. The nightmare reached out to grab him. Raoul's mind reeled, and then in a moment—all was black.

When Raoul awoke, he found himself in bed at the home of Christine's aunt. He called out for Christine, but her aunt assured the young count that she had left in the night.

"She did not know you were here. Why, the vicar found you only just this morning," said the old woman. "Thank the Lord you are all right."

"But where—where has she gone?" pleaded Raoul.

"Why, she left with him," the aunt said simply.

"Him? Who—tell me!" said Raoul with urgency.

"Why, she left with her *Angel of Music!*"

"Her what?! *Angel of Music?* Not that thing that played the violin last night!" said Raoul, half to himself.

"Most likely. The *Angel of Music* has given my Christine a voice from heaven. Though, I can't say it has brought her happiness. She so would have wanted to see you, Raoul, I am sure."

"Well, if that was her *Angel of Music,*" Raoul began as he climbed out of bed, "then he is an angel from below, not above." Raoul shuddered when he remembered the ghastly face he thought he saw through his dizzying eyes. Impossible, he thought. It must have been a dream. A trick of the light. Impossible!

Raoul made for Paris straightaway, but upon his return to the Opera, he found that Christine had still not returned. Where could she be? And with whom?

A whole week passed before Raoul was given even a clue. He had heard Christine had been seen riding in a black carriage through the streets of Paris for the last two nights. He dressed quickly and went out. It was bitterly cold. The road was lonely and deserted. He had walked for a good half hour when a carriage came quietly in his direction. As it approached, he saw that a woman was leaning her head from the window. And, suddenly, the moon shed a pale gleam over her features.

"Christine! Christine!" Raoul cried out.

No reply. The coach quickly disappeared from his sight.

Raoul received a letter the next day from Christine. It said:

RAOUL:

Go to the masked ball at the Opera on the night after tomorrow. Wear a white domino and be carefully masked. As you love me, do not let yourself be recognized. CHRISTINE.

The night of the ball came and Raoul did as he was commanded. Raoul leaned against a door post and waited. He did not wait long. A black domino passed and gave a quick squeeze to his hand. He understood it was she and followed her.

Christine moved swiftly through the party-goers as Raoul stayed right on her heels. That is, until she uttered a little cry, and turned suddenly in a different direction. Raoul stopped long enough to see what had frightened her. It was a man dressed all in scarlet, with a huge hat and feathers atop a wonderful death mask. From his shoulders hung an immense red cloak, embroidered with gold letters that read, "Don't touch me! I am Red Death stalking abroad!"

Raoul knew at once who the stranger was—he was the so called *Angel of Music.* He wanted to lay his hands on him, but Christine grabbed him by the arm and dragged him away at once.

"Don't try to stop me, Christine. I know who that is."

"No, you don't. You only think you know. I beg of you, stay away from him. He'll kill you without a second thought."

"I can take care of myself, Mademoiselle, I assure you. . . ."

"Don't be so foolish, Raoul; he might hear you!"

"Foolish!? Well, when you have a more civil tongue and care to tell me what this is all about—please do!" And Raoul turned quickly back into the crowd and left. Christine watched him leave for a moment and then went to her dressing room.

Everyone who saw Red Death that night knew who was really stalking. It was no ordinary man behind that skeleton's mask that night—it was the Opera Ghost himself!

Christine entered her dressing room frightened and exhausted. She collapsed into a chair and removed her mask. With her head in her hands she sighed, "Poor Erik!" Not for Raoul, not for herself, but for Erik! Who was Erik? If anyone had been around, the answer would have come swiftly. For a strange, faint singing could be heard coming from the walls . . . yes, as if the walls themselves were singing! She heard a voice, a very beautiful voice, soft and captivating. The voice came nearer and nearer, until it seemed the voice was right in the room. Christine rose from the chair and addressed the voice, as though speaking to someone:

"Here I am, Erik," she said. "I am ready. But you are late."

The voice without a body went on singing. The strains were unbelievably beautiful, heroic, and sweet. Christine walked to the far side of her room where the wall was entirely covered in mirrors. She reached out to touch her reflection, and in the next second the mirrors began to whirl about, taking Christine with them. When everything had once again returned to normal, Christine was gone! Growing fainter and fainter in the distance could be heard the voice, that sweet voice, as it slowly faded away and was gone, too, like the young Christine.

Raoul, it could be fairly said, brooded for the next two days. Finally realizing what a fool he had been, he dressed for the Opera and set off at once. He was determined to find Christine and ask her forgiveness and, if he could, discover her dark secret.

Raoul found Christine in her dressing room.

"Please, Christine, forgive me for my rude behavior. I promise—" Christine pressed her hand to Raoul's mouth to silence him. Then with a smile, she whispered, "Shhhh! We can't talk here. Follow me." She took Raoul by the hand and led him quietly from the room. They climbed up a flight of stairs, and then another, and then another, and still another. Finally, they found themselves high above the Opera stage.

"We'll be safe here—I hope," said Christine, trembling just a little. "He's working on his opera, and when he does, nothing else distracts him—sometimes for days."

"Now, tell me, Christine, what is this all about? Who is this Erik, or should I say *Angel of Music?* What possible hold could he have over you?"

"If I don't go to him when he wishes, terrible misfortunes will happen! And yet, he will call for me soon! I don't want to go! He will come and fetch me with his voice. And he will drag me with him, underground, and go on his knees before me, with his death's head. And he will tell me that he loves me! And he will cry! Oh, those tears, Raoul, those tears in the two black eye-sockets of the death's head! I cannot see those tears flow again!"

She wrung her hands in despair, while Raoul pressed her close to his heart.

"No, no, you shall never again hear him tell you that he loves you! You shall not see his tears! Let us fly, Christine, let us fly at once!"

"No, Raoul," she said, shaking her head sadly. "Not now! . . . It would be too cruel! Let him hear me sing tomorrow evening; then we will go away. You must come and fetch me in my dressing room at midnight exactly. He will be waiting for me at his house on the lake. We can escape then."

"Tell me—how did you come to know him?" Raoul asked.

"I heard him for the first three months without seeing him. His voice seemed to come out of thin air. And it not only sang, but it spoke to me and answered my questions, like a real man's voice, with this difference, that it was as beautiful as a voice of an angel. It said it was an angel, an angel of music, and that it would teach me how to sing just as sweetly. From that time on-ward, the voice and I became great friends. It asked leave to give me lessons every day. I agreed and never failed to keep the ap-pointment that it gave me in my dressing room. You have no

idea what those lessons were like. But you did hear the results."

"Oh, Christine," said Raoul, "my heart as well as every other who heard that night quivered at every accent of your voice."

"Raoul, it scared me so to hear such sounds from my mouth! And the voice made more and more demands upon my time. It followed me to Perros and played the violin at my father's grave. I know now you followed also, and saw the face—that horrid face that speaks like an angel."

"Yes, I saw the monster! How on earth could such beauty come from something so loathsome to look at?"

"He's capable of the greatest of evil, believe me," said Christine, shivering. "I'm sure he is responsible for dropping the chandelier on the audience that night."

"Why didn't you seek to escape from him?"

"I was afraid. Upon my return from Perros, he came for me. He wore a mask and refused to remove it. He took me by horse far below the Opera. You would not believe what lies under this house. There's a lake down there, and miles of corridors that wind and twist; how far down, I just don't know. He then took me by boat across the lake to a house he has built. It is a beautiful but sad place. He showed me where he sleeps in a coffin! Then he took me to a drawing room and kept me prisoner there for days! He only let me out for us to go on coach rides late at night. The drawing room is where he composes his opera; he calls it *Don Juan Triumphant*. He works tirelessly on it, day and night, at his dark organ. He begged me to love him, to make a whole man of him. I told him I would never love a man who keeps me prisoner! He said he had good reason to keep me shut up. Ah! and I soon found out that reason!"

"You saw him without his mask, no doubt!" cried Raoul.

"Yes, yes, though how I wish I hadn't!" Christine sighed. "He was giving me lessons, and his back was turned to me as he played the organ. I crept up slowly behind and pulled the mask

from his face! Oh, the horror! Red Death's mask suddenly coming to life with the four black holes of its eyes, its nose, and its mouth. Oh, the anger, the mighty fury of a demon; *and not a ray of light from its sockets*, for, as I learned later, you cannot see his blazing eyes except in the dark.

"I fell back against the wall and he came up to me, grinding his teeth, and, as I fell to my knees, he shouted mad, incoherent words and curses at me. Leaning over me, he cried, 'Look! You want to see! See! Feast your eyes, glut your soul on my cursed ugliness! Look at Erik's face! Now you know the face behind the voice! You were not content to hear me, eh? Well, are you satisfied? I'm a very good-looking fellow, eh? . . . When a woman has seen me, as you have, she belongs to me. She loves me forever. I am a kind of Don Juan, don't you think?' I screamed and fainted. When I awoke, he had replaced his mask, and was busy with his opera."

"How on earth did you ever escape such a prison?"

"He kept begging me for my love, despite his appearance, and crying, oh, such wailing you have never heard! I finally convinced him to let me return with the promise I would come again. He said if I broke my word he would kill me and many many others. So, I have returned to him as he has asked, but no more. No more!"

"Don't worry," Raoul said kindly. "I'll make all the arrangements for our trip. Two nights from now we will be far far away from here." And he held her close.

But the two lovers had not gone unnoticed altogether. Oh, no, not by any means. A shadow moved away quickly as they made their way back down to the stage.

Raoul spent all the next day arranging for train passage, a carriage, and seeing that their baggage would be properly taken care of. Christine had spent the day resting before her performance that night. Nothing out of the ordinary happened all day.

That night Raoul arrived at the Opera by carriage. The carriage was packed and ready to leave at a moment's notice. He felt confident everything was in order for their midnight flight. He didn't know it as he sat down in his box for the night's performance, but he was wrong. Very, very wrong.

The Opera was once again giving a performance of *Faust*, with Christine as the beautiful Margarita. Christine was giving the performance of a lifetime. She stood on stage, her arms outstretched, her throat filled with music, the glory of her hair over her bare shoulders, as she uttered a divine song.

It was at that moment that the stage was suddenly plunged in darkness. It happened so quickly that the spectators hardly had time to utter a sound of surprise, for the gas at once lit up the stage again. But Christine Daae was no longer there!

Where had Christine gone? What witchcraft had snatched her away before the eyes of thousands of onlookers? Raoul wasted no time, and made for Christine's dressing room straightaway.

When he reached the dressing room a crowd had already gathered. The managers had arrived along with an inspector of police who happened to be in attendance that night. Raoul was the last to enter. As he was about to follow the rest into the room, a hand was laid on his shoulder, and he heard these words spoken in his ear: *"Erik's secrets concern no one but himself!"*

He turned around, with a stifled cry. The hand that was laid on his shoulder was now placed on the lips of a person with ebony skin, with eyes of jade and with an astrakhan cap on his head. The person was called the Persian. Raoul had heard of him many times, as the Persian was in regular attendance at the Opera over the last several months.

The stranger kept up the gesture that cautioned silence, and then, at the moment the young count was about to ask the reason for his mysterious intervention, he bowed and disappeared. Raoul proceeded inside with the others, more confused than ever.

Once inside Christine's dressing room, the inspector asked Raoul to have a seat.

"I have been given to understand by these gentlemen, sir, that you are a particular favorite of Christine Daae. Can you shed any light upon her disappearance this evening?"

"We were . . . were to leave together this very night. I have a carriage packed and waiting in front of the Opera. We would be away from here by now if . . . if he had not taken her."

"He? Who is he, sir?" said the inspector with keen interest.

"Why, the Opera Ghost, of course. Or if you prefer, the Angel of Music, or better yet his name, Erik. Yes, Erik would be better! Whatever, he has taken her underground and we must go after them," stammered out Raoul.

When the managers heard the name "Opera Ghost" they were a little taken aback. Since that night the chandelier had fallen, they had made the payments demanded by the ghost. But kidnapping their star singer? Impossible! They looked at the inspector as if to say, "Surely you can see the young man is overwrought with emotion!" The inspector saw it that way also.

"I assure you, sir, we will do everything possible to find the young lady," said the inspector. "Now please, if you would wait outside while I question the managers further on this matter."

Raoul did as he was told, seeing that no one in that room believed a word he had to say. But Raoul was quickly set upon by the Persian again, just outside the door. He led him away down the hall and into another dressing room.

"I hope, young count," he said, "that you have not betrayed Erik's secret?"

"And why should I hesitate to betray that monster, sir?" Raoul said haughtily, trying to shake off the intruder. "Is he your friend, by any chance?"

"I hope you said nothing about Erik, sir, because Erik's secret is also Mademoiselle Daae's, and to talk about one is to talk

about the other!"

"Sir, you seem to know about many things that interest me; and yet I have no time to listen to you!"

"Where are you going so fast, young count?"

"Can you not guess? To Christine Daae's assistance . . ."

"Then, sir, stay here, for Christine Daae is here!"

"With Erik?"

"With Erik."

"How do you know?"

"I was at the performance, and no one in the world but Erik could contrive an abduction like that! Oh," he said, with a deep sigh, "I recognized the monster's touch!"

"You know him then?"

"I know him well. I can aid you now, sir, and take you to where he is. But you must put your complete trust in me, or we shall both perish this night. You have no idea what kind of evil genius we are up against."

"If you can help free Christine, I am completely at your disposal. Command me."

The Persian opened a small case and pulled out two loaded pistols, giving one to Raoul.

"We shall do all that is humanly possible to do! But he may stop us at the very first step! He commands the walls, the doors, and even the trap-doors! In my country, he was known by a name that means the 'trap-door lover.'"

"But why do these walls obey him alone? He did not build them," said Raoul, puzzled.

"Yes, sir, that is just what he did!"

The Persian motioned Raoul to be silent and to follow him. "We must go down Erik's road. I beg you to be silent and do what I do or else we shall be undone!" Raoul nodded in agreement and followed closely behind the Persian as he wound his way down staircase after staircase, and hallway after hallway.

When they had reached some three stories below the Opera, the Persian froze and flattened himself against the wall. Raoul did the same in turn. He could hear a scratching, scraping, grating sound coming toward them. In the next moment, to their horror, a head—a head of fire—was coming straight for them.

The Persian and Raoul could retreat no farther and flattened themselves as best they could against the wall. The sound was made up of hundreds of little sounds that moved in the darkness, under the fiery face.

The fiery head came closer and closer. Raoul and the Persian were ready to faint, but the head turned to them and spoke: "Don't move! Don't move! Whatever you do, don't come after me! I am the rat-catcher! Let me pass, with my rats!"

And the head of fire disappeared, vanishing in the darkness. The passage in front lit up as the rat-catcher jumped along, dragging with him the waves of scratching rats, all the thousand sounds.

Raoul and the Persian breathed again, though still trembling.

"I ought to have remembered that Erik talked to me about the rat-catcher," said the Persian. "But he never told me that he looked like that! It's funny I should not have met him before. Of course, Erik never comes to this part of the Opera!"

"Christine said Erik had his house on a lake. Are we near the lake now? How will we cross? By boat?" asked Raoul impatiently.

"We shall never enter the house on the lake by the lake!" said the Persian. "I myself have never landed on the other bank . . . the bank on which the house stands. You have to cross the lake first, and it is well guarded! I fear that more than one of those men—old scene-shifters, old door-shutters—who have never been seen again were simply tempted to cross the lake and have a look for themselves. It is terrible! I myself would have been nearly killed there if the monster had not recognized me in time!"

"What do you mean?" asked Raoul, quite puzzled.

"One day, when I thought myself alone, I stepped into a boat and began rowing toward the house. As I approached the middle of the lake I began to hear a voice. The voice seemed to be everywhere, and yet nowhere. Little by little I found that the voice was in the water. I leaned over the side of the boat, and as I did so, two monstrous arms jumped from the water and seized me by the neck. I certainly would have been dragged down into the water if Erik had not recognized me just in time. 'How imprudent you are!' he said. 'Why try to enter my house? I never invited you! I don't want you there, nor anybody! You saved my life once; that I have not forgotten. But I may end this by forgetting it; and you know that nothing can restrain me, not even myself.'

"I knew all too well what he meant, having seen the depth of his cruelty when he lived in my country. But it was true; I did save his life once. He had even promised me that he would not commit murder again. But I know Erik all too well, and I followed him from my country to here, hoping for the chance to end his reign of terror—half-hoping he would be a different person. You see, Erik deserves a measure of pity. He has had to live with the most horrible of deformities from the time of his birth, and it has affected him in no small measure. He let me go that day, and for him, I pray it will be his undoing!"

"If we can't enter his house by the lake, how do you propose we get there?" asked Raoul.

"We are on the third level," the Persian began. "The lake is directly below us now. I have seen Erik enter his house by a trap-door on this level. We shall do the same, if the monster is not wise to our presence! Hurry now; we haven't a moment to lose!"

Raoul followed the Persian as he made his way through what seemed an endless number of twisting, turning passageways. At last the Persian stopped, and signaled to Raoul that they were

now over the house of the Opera ghost. It soon became apparent that the monster was at home, for they could hear him speaking below in a passionate voice:

"You must make your choice! The wedding mass or the requiem mass! The requiem mass is not at all gay, whereas the wedding mass—you can take my word for it—is magnificent! You must decide! I can't go on living like this, like a mole in a burrow! *Don Juan Triumphant* is finished; and now I want to live like everybody else. I want to have a wife like everybody else and to take her out on Sundays. I have invented a mask that makes me look like anybody. People will not even turn round in the streets. You will be the happiest of women. And we will sing, all by ourselves, till we faint away with delight. You are crying! You are afraid of me! And yet I am not really wicked. Love me and you shall see! All I wanted was to be loved for myself. If you loved me I should be as gentle as a lamb; and you could do anything with me that you pleased."

Raoul and the Persian both gave a shudder at the sounds they heard next. For there arose such moans of anguish and despair than have ever been heard. They realized the cries of pain were from the monster himself. Erik had fallen to his knees before Christine, who had not the strength to cry out.

In the ill-lit passage above, Raoul knocked against an old stage prop and sent it crashing to the floor.

"Someone visits Erik's house uninvited?" the monster's voice could be heard to say.

The Persian quickly motioned to Raoul to follow him back down the passage. They concealed themselves just as the trap-door flew open and the ghost rose up through the floor. He remained there, silent—listening—for what seemed like an eternity to our two heroes. But at last he went back down, slamming the trap-door shut behind him.

"Only rats, my dear, only rats," Erik said. "Now, decide! You

hold the fate of our lives this night! I shall leave you to decide. If you are to be my wife, turn the scorpion round. If your answer is 'no,' then turn the grasshopper round." And Erik showed Christine the two golden creatures placed on the mantelpiece. Then he laughed like a drunken demon, and said, "The grasshopper! Be careful of the grasshopper! The grasshopper does not only turn: it hops! It hops! And it hops jolly high!"

Raoul heard the Persian sound a sad moan at these words.

"Oh, no, he would not!" The Persian said to himself.

"What? What does this all mean?" Raoul demanded.

"The grasshopper! She must not turn the grasshopper! As of late Erik has been gathering barrels down by the lake. I know of his love of wine, so I didn't give it a second thought. But now, the grasshopper! The grasshopper will hop, and I fear a goodly number of people with it! Those barrels must be full of gunpowder, not wine! If he can't have his beloved Christine, I'm sure he means to blow up the Opera! We must act quickly!"

The ghost had left Christine alone in the drawing-room to decide. The Persian wasted no time in opening the trap-door and dropping safely into the room. Raoul followed close behind.

"Whatever you do, please don't touch that grasshopper!"

"Raoul! You have come! Oh, what are we to do! He's quite mad and . . ." But Christine did not have time to finish, for Erik had returned.

He crept up behind Raoul and gave him a hard blow to the back of his head, knocking him out immediately.

"I warned you not to meddle in my affairs!" the ghost screamed at the Persian. "You have crossed me for the last time, my friend, and now you shall pay dearly for this intrusion. You shall all pay, do you hear? Erik will not be denied! Erik is always denied!"

But the monster did not step forward to turn the grasshopper like he planned. He would have except for a soft moan that

came to his ears. He turned to see Christine crying and holding the stricken Raoul. She looked up at him, tears filling her deep blue eyes, and said:

"You monster! All you care about is yourself! I hate you! How can you expect anyone to love you? You have not a shred of love in you, of common decency. It is not your face that is monstrous, but your heart! Go ahead, kill us all! I will never love you! I loathe you for the hateful creature you are!" And Christine broke down in dreadful sobs.

The monster had been struck straight through the heart. He staggered back under the weight of her words. His head hung low, he spoke to the Persian in slow, sad tones:

"Go, my friend, and take them with you. Erik is very tired. So very tired, indeed. Christine, I only . . ." But he didn't finish his words to her.

"You will not harm the Opera, Erik?" the Persian asked.

"No. Now go, before Erik changes his mind!"

The Persian gathered up the fallen Raoul and began to leave at once. Christine started to follow, but stopped, and ran back to Erik. With tears flowing from her eyes, she hugged him, and whispered softly, "I'm so sorry, Erik, I'm so very, very sorry. Ah, poor, unhappy Erik." Then the three departed by boat across the lake. Erik watched in silence as they disappeared into the dark.

A week later the Persian had a visitor to his flat. It was Erik.

"I have come to you, my friend, to tell you that I am dying. But before I die I wanted you to know something. The day I released you and your companions I too was released. When Christine came back and told me she was sorry—sorry for me— I was changed. She hugged me and wept for me. I felt her tears flow on my forehead . . . on mine, mine! They were soft, they were sweet! They trickled under my mask . . . they mingled with my tears in my eyes . . . they flowed between my lips! We cried together! She whispered sweetly, *'Poor, unhappy Erik!'* I have

tasted all the happiness the world can offer! I am happy she is going to marry that young man, because I was ready to die for her and she had taken pity on me! She has cried with me and mingled her tears with mine! I could not expect anything more."

No one could have doubted the word of the weeping Erik that night.

The Persian had seen the poor, unfortunate Erik for the last time. Three weeks later, the Paris paper published this advertisement: "Erik is dead."

The Persian discovered that Christine had gone to Erik's side during his final days, and had arranged for his burial at his passing. It was she who had placed the advertisement. It was she who had cared. In the end, for the Phantom of the Opera, it was Christine—nothing else. It was *always* Christine.

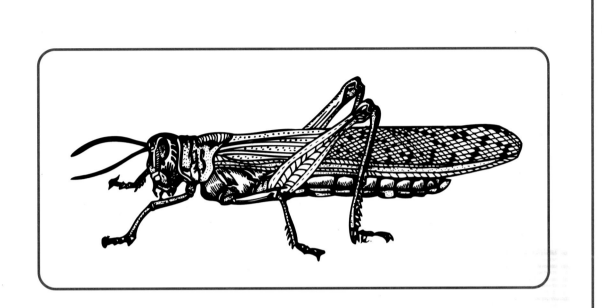

Copyright © 1993 by The Unicorn Publishing House
Artwork © 1988 by Greg Hildebrandt
This edition published by Barnes & Noble, Inc.,
by arrangement with Greg Hildebrandt
All rights reserved
No part of this book may be used or reproduced in any
manner whatsoever without the written permission of the Publisher.
1996 Barnes & Noble Books
ISBN 0-7607-0378-7
Printed and bound in the United States of America
M 9 8 7 6 5 4 3 2 1
KP